P9-DWD-834

An I Can Read Book™

STORY AND PICTURES BY

HarperCollins*Publishers*

Space Cat

www.harperchildrens.com

Library of Congress Cataloging-in-Publication Data
Cushman, Doug.
Space cat / story and pictures by Doug Cushman.
p. cm. — (An I can read book)
Summary: When Space Cat and Earl the robot encounter trouble with their space ship, they crash-land on an alien planet to search for more fuel.
ISBN 0-06-008965-2 — ISBN 0-06-008966-0 (lib. bdg.)
[1. Cats—Fiction. 2. Robots—Fiction. 3. Science fiction.] I. Title. II. Series.
PZ7.C959Sp 2004
[E]—dc21
2003008730

---

1 2 3 4 5 6 7 8 9 10

First Edition

To Fritz Lang, Flash Gordon,
and the crew of the *Starship Enterprise*

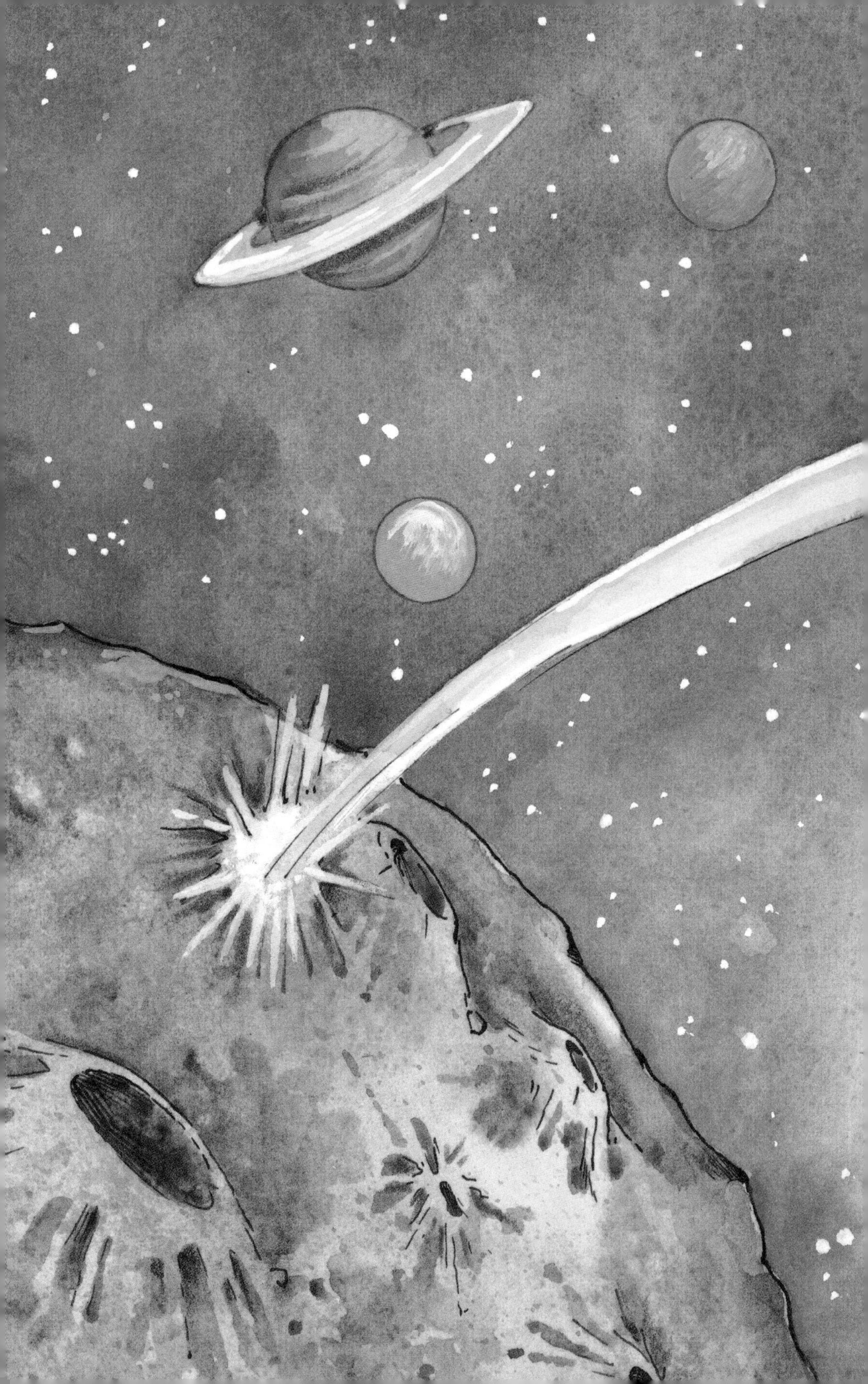

BLAM!

WHOOSH!

Space Cat took off in his rocket.

He was flying home to Earth.

“I’m hungry,” said Space Cat.

“My fish and jelly noodles

will be ready soon,”

said Earl the robot.

"You don't know how to cook,"

said Space Cat.

"The last time you made noodles,

they tasted like glue!"

"A robot never gives up,"

said Earl.

Suddenly there was a

CRASH!

Red lights flashed

and buzzers buzzed.

“What was that?” asked Space Cat.

“It was a space rock,” said Earl.

“It hit our rocket

and made a hole

in the fuel tank.

We will run out of fuel soon.”

"I see a planet ahead,"

said Space Cat.

"We can land there to fix our rocket."

Space Cat landed safely

on the planet.

"I'll go outside

and look for some fuel," he said.

"I will stay here

and fix the fuel tank," said Earl.

"Then I will fix dinner.

A robot never gives up."

Space Cat walked outside.

He saw a big city ahead.

"I'll look for some fuel there,"

he said.

Space Cat came to the city.

He saw many strange creatures.

“Excuse me,” he said.

“I need some rocket fuel.

Can you help me?”

“King Zorp has all the fuel,”

said a creature.

“He lives in that big castle.”

Space Cat went to the castle
and knocked on the big door.
A guard opened it.
"Please help me," said Space Cat.
"I need some fuel to get home."
"Follow me to the king's room,"
said the guard.

They walked into a big room.

"I am King Zorp!"

said a big creature on a throne.

"What do you want?"

"A space rock hit my rocket,"

said Space Cat.

"My rocket fuel is all gone.

I need some more to get home."

"Sorry," said King Zorp.

"I need all the fuel on this planet.

I am a big king with big plans!

And my plans need lots of fuel!"

"But how can I leave

without rocket fuel?"

asked Space Cat.

"I must go home!"

"Well, I guess you are stuck here,"

said King Zorp.

"This is not a bad planet,"

said King Zorp.

"The people are nice.

The food is good.

Let me show you around."

King Zorp took Space Cat

into another big room.

He pushed a button.

BUZZ! CLANK! CLANK!

The machines rattled and puffed.

The room rumbled

with all the noise.

“These machines

are part of my big plans,”

said King Zorp.

“This one helps clean the water.

That one cleans the air.

All my machines need lots of fuel.

That is why you cannot have

even one drop.”

The room rumbled louder.

“But I can’t stay,” said Space Cat.

“I must go home. I . . .”

Space Cat stopped.

CLANK! CLANK! BUZZ!

The room began to shake.

The machines puffed and rattled
louder and louder.
Screws and bolts fell to the floor.
"My machines are falling apart!"
cried King Zorp.

Suddenly the door opened.

"Hello, Space Cat," said Earl.

He was holding a bowl of noodles.

"I was looking for you," he said.

"I fixed the fuel tank.

Now I am making the noodles.

But I can't find the ketchup."

CRACK!

“Look out!” cried King Zorp.

“That machine is coming loose!”

Space Cat grabbed the bowl

from Earl.

He threw it at the machine.

SPLAT!

Noodles dripped from the bowl.

They covered the machine

and the wall.

The machine was stuck.

It did not fall.

“How did you know
those noodles would do that?”
asked King Zorp.
“Earl’s noodles taste like glue,”
said Space Cat.
“So I thought they would also
stick like glue.”
“How can I thank you?”
asked King Zorp.
“Please give me a little fuel
for my rocket,” said Space Cat.
“With pleasure!” said King Zorp.

Space Cat took some fuel

back to his rocket.

BLAM!

WHOOSH!

The rocket took off.

“I’m still hungry,” said Space Cat.

“Good,” said Earl.

“I am making

some spaghetti and meatballs.

They are in the toaster now.”

“It’s going to be
a long trip home,”
said Space Cat.